MAKING

WINGS

Short Stories and Poems

C. Nathaniel Brown

EXPECTED END

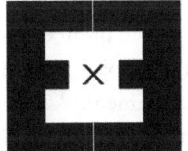

ENTERTAINMENT

Atlanta, GA

Published by Expected End Entertainment/EX3 Books
Library of Congress Control Number: 2014915010
ISBN: 0988554585
ISBN-13: 978-0-9885545-8-0
Printed in the United States of America

DEDICATION

This book is dedicated to my angels, Minnie Brown (Granny) and Gloria Kemp (Mom), and to my mother, Ellen Brown.

CONTENTS

INTRODUCTION

I've always had a passion for writing, especially creative writing because it offered an escape from the realities in which I lived. That's not to say that it was all bad, but I enjoyed being able to express myself through my pen and introduce a new world that I had yet to experience.

I remember reading the poetry of Langston Hughes, Paul Laurence Dunbar, and Maya Angelou and trying to write poems using the same styles. I'd read stories by Zora Neal Hurston and Ralph Ellison and believe that I could engage readers with the stories that occupied my head. I loved spending time in the library and bookstores imagining what my book covers would look like one day.

In college, one of my professors told me I would never become a professional writer and that I should consider another career path. But two other professors at Denison University encouraged me to write – Dr. Jack Kirby and Dr. David Baker, one of the best poets I ever encountered. I continued to write poems, stories, ideas, movie scenes, jokes, and just about anything else I could think of.

I published my first book, I Always Put the Seat Down, in 1996 (After reading a history paper with that title my senior year, Dr. Kirby suggested I used it for my first book). It was one of the biggest accomplishments of my life at that point because I was living a dream. The day I walked into a bookstore to host a reading and autograph signing session and saw my book on display right beside Maya Angelou's books, I knew that I could achieve anything I dreamt utilizing my writing.

Having worked more than 20 years as a journalist, authored

six books, written dozens of screenplays, and participated in several other writing collaborations, I am proud to say I am living my dream. But for me, that's not enough. That's why I have set out to help 10,000 writers get published.

As you read Making Wings, which I dedicate to the memory of my two biggest cheerleaders, my grandmother, Minnie Brown, and my mother in-law, Gloria Kemp, and to my mother, Ellen Brown, who has always told me I could be and do anything my heart desired regardless of the circumstances, I hope that you are encouraged, inspired and motivated to speak your dreams, pursue your dreams, and live your dreams.

I know that our paths will cross again. Much love!

C. Nathaniel Brown
"Chuck"

POEMS

MAKING WINGS (POEM)

(For Granny and Mom)

An eagle soars above me in the distance.

My mind glides to that peace where sunsets are born.

You were there. You were the sunset.

You are here. I miss you today.

Just as I did yesterday.

And the day before.

When the sun rises, I smile.

You were there. You were the sunrise.

You are my sunrise today, despite the rain.

I'll take that breeze as a sign.

You are here.

I look up and see your wings.

I soar because of them.

Because of you.

I was there. I am here.

Thank you!

IT DOESN'T MATTER

Pitter patter.

It doesn't matter.

Take the sooner.

Or the latter.

Choose the skinny.

Or the fatter.

Either way,

It doesn't matter.

SMILE

Smile.

Open the blinds of fortune.

Breathe the breath of God's child.

For he has birthed you and blessed you with his presence.

DROUGHT

The sun screamed in our ears.

Our bodies responded inside.

Pain and suffering bellowed outside.

But no rain would fall.

5th SEASON (III)

Winter.

Spring.

Summer.

Fall.

You.

CATCH 22

So there's a treasure at the end of the rainbow?

Why does it go on and on?

I can never seem to reach its end.

When it appears that I'm close, it disappears.

ON THE WALL

On the wall I sit,

    For one reason and one reason alone,

For when I cannot grace your presence,

    Or cannot be reached by phone.

Just look up and see my face,

    And know that I'm there with you,

To offer a smile, a wink or two,

    Whenever you're feeling blue.

So when the load gets heavy,

    And on occasion you stumble and fall,

There will always be that "pick-me-up" –

    My picture on the wall.

WHAT IS LOVE?

Is love things expressed in different ways?
Is love that twinkle in a lover's gaze?

Is love the things you always wanted but never received?
Is love that simple feeling of tears watching her leave?

Is love that special something that causes a random smile?
Is love that connection you share despite distances of miles?

Is love the feeling of butterflies when someone mentions your name?
Is love that fine line of love where pleasure meets pain?

Is love that thing that some call easy and some call extremely hard?
Is love the blessing we receive from Almighty God?

Is love the smell of your perfume even though I know you're not there?
Is love the public affection you share any and everywhere?

Is love that thing they say money can't buy?
Is love that ever-present feeling of being sky high?

Is love that refreshing that turns grey skies blue?
All I know is... I love defining love with you.

19

EXTENSION

The torch of external life

ignited from the sparkle

of her eyes.

Her smooth ebony skin

melted into his rugged flesh

to create the beautiful hour glass figure.

The lights shadowed the joyous emotions

onto the floor.

Her hair flowed calmly,

like the Nile.

His eyes swam the banks

of her waters

until he, too, calmly flowed.

They continued a legacy of pride.

20

JUST YOUR SHADOW

"It's just your shadow," I'd say,

but still she'd run and scream.

She acted as if it were a boogieman,

straight from her worst dream.

She'd grab a hold and squeeze me tight,

and would not let me go.

She'd look around to make sure it was gone

and then she'd let me know.

I'd put her down, she'd start to walk

and then that "thing" reappeared.

I didn't think there was a thing in the world

that this little girl feared.

So we stopped and waved hi and later goodbye,

but before that we played a few games.

We made doggie faces and birds in high places,

unfortunately the fear remained the same.

She was really afraid when she was alone

and had to face it one-on-one.

Playing outside was an issue for her,

it wasn't fun in the sun.

So I reversed the roles and faked a cry

and told her it was that "thing" that I feared.

She held my hand, said, "Daddy, don't cry.

It's just your shadow. Don't be scared."

SILLY

People say they don't understand you. Frankly, I don't

either. Do they wish to? Do I? They like to deflect your

most sincere opinions, but would much rather stay totally

away. I like to be around you and laugh at those silly

thoughts.

SHE ATE IT UP

Smiles introduced us from a distance.

Our eyes pulled us together.

As I whispered sweet nothings in her ear,

She began to undress me with her eyes.

I felt her nibbling.

Soon after, she began to stroke me.

It must have been an eternity since she's eaten

Because she was extremely hungry.

Being the gentleman I am,

I continued to feed her

And quench that curiosity of thirst.

I filled her up until I realized

I was making love to her mind.

ONE-OF-A-KIND

Like suction cups to glass, my eyes transfixed the golden

brown legs with curves like a Rogers Clemons special.

Movement in a near-rehearsed manner, certainly poetry in

motion. I could dance to the rhythm as I watched them

dance away. One of a kind, unmistakable, identical to

none. I'd know them if I ever saw them again.

BRANDY

Brandy got him through the night.

Whenever waves became overbearing,

He turned to her.

Sure as the morning sun, she was there.

She was strong, and inside, warm.

He found himself becoming one with her.

No longer just during trouble times.

He made a commitment to her.

Every free second belonged to her.

She, however, was no longer a solution

But a problem.

Brandy led him to another commitment.

Because of anonymity, I can only give her initials –

A.A.

STRENGTH

I think!

Therefore I'm a rational being.

I rebel!

Change is the only constant in life.

I reflect!

Knowing what I had, I still have.

I forgive!

We move forward together, not apart.

I learn!

Knowledge is the key to success.

I succeed!

I'm a strong black man with ancestors on my back

And our future on my shoulders.

MY FEATHERED FRIEND

One morning I woke to the sound of chirping. I managed my way to the window. The morning sun temporarily blinded me.

Through squinted eyes I saw my feathered friend, the earliest bird, nestled next to another. It was there, singing the sweetest song one could imagine.

Morning after morning, I woke to that song, sang by my feathered friend. Until one morning there was no singing, there was no bird, and ironically, there was no sun.

Never again did I see my feathered friend or hear that sweet song. So I named her Memory and the song, 'Gone'.

MY MOTHER, MY FRIEND

Though a mother's job is never done

and her worries seems never to end.

She does receive some retribution

when she finds her child is her friend.

When the two are able to share things

that normally would not be known,

The love between them is realized

it's not always said, but it's always shown.

The pride that she has for things he's done

that to him is not much at all.

To her they're reflections of things she's taught

that he's finally learned after all.

One would have to live at least five times

to repay her for all her love and care.

Her time, her patience and most of all

for simply being there.

I know that she gives lots of love

and often spreads herself thin.

But this bit of love and thanks to her

is for being my mother and my friend.

MY HIGH

On Cloud 9.

I lay on my back always looking up.

Call optimism a drug of choice.

I try to share the way I feel.

I tell others that being high (my way) is loving themselves,

Not shooting, smoking, or sniffing.

NOTIONS OF INNOCENCE

Fingers sought speech

But discovered silence.

Minds conceived actions,

But soles secured immobility.

Shadows of doubt clouded my dreams.

I was neither thought of nor heard of.

FATHER, FATHER

In times of trouble and distress

I know you are always there.

But Father, Father,

Sometimes I just need you here!

SWEET SWEAT

Sweet sweat came thundering down my face,

Eroding the coal through my pores,

Causing hot and cold flashes,

Congratulating me on a job well done.

MY SHADOW

Side by side, we wandered the paths of the park.

I was thinking how lonely I was

and he was thinking how nice it was to have company.

My pace increased as my bags filled with tears.

Nothing seemed to be a part of me.

So I looked to the ground,

found a spot under a tree,

and became one with my shadow.

MY, MY, MY

I bathed in the sunshine of her personality.

My eyes felt her where only imaginations should.

My first impression was my second...

Third... and final impressions.

My heart sank as if she had dropped an anchor

To immobilize me.

I walked a tightrope of friendliness

Without a net to fall back on.

I held fast to the morning glow that cast about me.

My mind clawed at the lock of my attention.

To no avail.

GLARING STARE

I watched those eyes as they watched me.

Sparkles shot out that only I could see.

It set off a rainbow of colors brightly lit.

So I basked in its warmth and relaxed just a bit.

From there I witnessed the difference in between.

It hardly mattered after what had been seen.

I shaded my eyes from the glare that seeped through.

But saved enough space to still peek at you.

Now I'm looking far beyond those eyes.

And feel comfort that relaxes butterflies.

My mind and soul are both at ease.

And that glaring stare is a summer breeze.

LONELY BIRD

A lonely bird is one who flies without a place to go.
And when the sun rises he sets off to a place he has yet to
know.

Then it is said that he is heard singing a morning song.
Truth to this is that he cries as he wanders along.

He wanders out in search of food, a nest, a home, a friend.
All he finds is hard times and the day is about to end.

As the sun begins to set and it's halfway to the west.
All the lonely bird has found is that he needs his rest.

He heads back to a nest that he calls his home.
It took him a while to realize that he was still alone.

He shook his feathers, thought of sleep and then began to
pray.
"Dear Lord, help me survive this life and find happiness if I
may.

I'll try my best tomorrow to live it safely through.
Until I reach the Golden Gate and head home to you.
Amen."

AIRBORNE

Wandering the park,

I came across a nest of shade.

For minutes it became my home.

I ate. I slept. I dreamt. I woke.

I smelled the blossoming flowers

And they hummed a tune with the birds.

I gazed at the surroundings

And my mind took to flight,

As thoughts rode the wings of the wind.

SUGAR CUBE

Our eyes absorbed the moisture of each other's. First eye contact magnetized superficial intentions. Wind whistles fragrances of your person. You glide down the aisle towards me. It takes an eternity, but my enjoyment plateaus at that everlasting moment. Incidental contact struck confusion within me, for I knew not whether it truly was "incidental".

Patience, nervousness, and the like, numbed my memory of speech. Those lips cured that amnesia by chance. Broken ice is now behind me. I awake with anticipations of sweetness.

DILEMMA

To love you and not be able to have you.

OR

Not to love you and not be able to have you.

STORM WINDOW

Nothing separated me from the violent storm but a curtainless window.

Thunder screamed and lightning lit the sky with a sarcastic grin, in retaliation.

The sky spat upon everything on the other side of the window.

Cars cried and wiped away tears as fast as they could. People shielded with umbrellas laughed at those without, while angry cars splashed them all.

Trees tried to shake the wetness away but wet each other instead.

The jealous sun fought its way out until stubborn clouds swallowed it up and coughed out giant-sized hail that crashed down on buildings, buses and people.

I was protected on the other side by the storm window.

BLOWN AWAY

The smallest of swaying trees

Bowed down to greet me.

I laughed at their boney limbs,

Although I acknowledged their

Performance with applause.

Even the tiniest arms have

Huge comfort in their hugs.

EYES IN THE 2nd STORY WINDOW

Piercing eyes stared inside my 2nd story window. Fright escalated above the ceiling.

Sleep sneaked out the immediacy of my mind. I possessed a weapon to defend myself from this evil.

Who or what had entered fear into my fearless heart? Surely nothing was suspended in mid-air.

Was I afraid of what tomorrow would bring? Had I been thinking of my mistakes?

Or were they my eyes that I looked into?

LETTER TO DESTINY

Destiny,

I fail to believe the best things in life are free. Since Day 1, I've been paying the dear price of pain. My motivation is my strong belief that nothing worth having is ever easy. Faith has shown me the ups and downs of life. Sometimes it's not such an easy ride and I must walk, but the results are gratifying. Dedication and determination will lend hands in sincere quests. Therefeore, my obstacles are bridges to cross not crosses to bear.

My mind has been on strike to all other thoughts. I see the bigger picture, beautifully. The artist? My mind... carefully stroking feelings onto my canvas heart. If patience is a virtue, I'll wait for that portrait to be completed.

Destiny, when we're both able to look at the larger picture, we'll share its joy, happiness and love forever. Then we'll reflect (and laugh) at the cloudy past behind us as we grow together in the everlasting sunshine.

Love,

Me

FIRST STAR

No more time for summer flings.

Time to search for lasting things.

Only when I can say goodbye.

I'll find a love that'll never die.

So, First Star, I see above,

I wish for everlasting love.

So on this clear summer night,

I start my search for a love out-of-sight.

DRAIN OPENER

In darkness's eyes, I outlined my love for you as you lay, curled against my sheets.

Your wetness, my bath, sprinkled clean images of a fonder fire beneath my cap.

Those caressed brown… golden brown… now black features honeyed bits of sweetness to my buds.

I slithered around to avoid disruption of your determined state. Harvested in mid-night's furniture, the silhouette drained.

DIRTY OLD MAN

I.   There was an old man in a suit.
      He warned that he would poot.
      They paid him no mind.
      And out of his behind,
      Came a fart that knocked off his boot.

II.   They heard the sound it made.
      They hated the game he played.
      They whiffed a smell,
      Couldn't help but yell,
      As the man took a seat in the shade.

SHINING STAR

If I caught a fallen star, this is what I'd do.
I'd fling it back into space and name it after you.

I'd visit you every night, blowing kisses to the sky.
I'd feel your glow and warm embrace, a presence
undenied.

I'd remember every kiss you gave, every hug and every
word.
I'd remember every wise advice, and every, "I Love you,"
that I heard.

And when the time comes to say goodbye, I'd wink and
say goodnight.
Until tomorrow's meeting, Shining Star, sweet dreams,
now rest your light.

PHENOMENAL ME

I tried being who others wanted me to be.

And not only did I fail, I became something

no one wanted me to be

and ended up in a place I never wanted to be.

So I made a commitment to God

to be the best me HE wanted me to be.

And so far I'm liking that me.

And the me I see I am becoming...

Wow!

That's PHENOMENAL ME!"

SHORT STORIES

MY ANNABEL LEE

I'll never forget watching her watching step down off the bus. I know there were dozens of other high school students our age all around her. But for that minute, that moment in time, it was only her, as if she were gliding on a cloud towards me. She had on a pair of blue jean shorts, a pink t-shirt and a pair of sandals. She carried a small, pink gym bag over her shoulder. But in my mind she was wearing a white, strapless wedding gown with shining beads of some kind down the front. She had the prettiest bouquet I had ever seen, not that I had seen many. Our eyes fixed and we smiled at each other as she got close enough for me to extend my hand for hers.

"Zack! Zack!" my friend, Carl, yelled, breaking me from the most perfect 30 seconds of my life at that point. "Com'on, they're taking us to our cabin." He grabbed my arm and pulled me away. I looked back and she and her friends were walking away, down a path towards another cabin. I watched as long as I could but Carl - being Carl - kept me distracted.

"This is going to be the best summer camp ever," Carl said, as we caught up to Joey and Sticks. "I can't wait to go swimming and fishing."

"Are there bears out here? If so, I'm sleeping with one eye open," Joey said.

"Shut up, chicken!" Carl said.

We all laughed.

I look back again for her but I could no longer see her. For a split second, I wondered if I only imagined her. And just like that, it came out... "My poem!"

"What!?!" Joey said.

"Nothing." I said.

"We are about to have the time of our lives and you are talking about writing poetry?" Carl quipped, pushing me and clowning with the others. "I don't know what's wrong with this boy."

"He misses his mommy," Sticks joked.

I laughed but I knew they wouldn't understand. I looked back again hoping I would see her. Carl spotted our group and we caught up to them and went into our cabin with Antonio, our camp counselor. It looked like something out of a movie or a TV show where people were killed in the middle of the night. There was a fireplace in the living room and huge ceilings. There was a long table in the middle of the floor with about 20 chairs around it. I guess that's where we'll all eat. I started wondering if we would roast marshmellows or go hunting or eat the fish we caught. It was my first time at camp so my mind was going to everything I had seen on TV. But it would always find its way back to her.

As we made our way up the stairs to our rooms, I looked out the windows somehow hoping she'd be walking past even though the girls cabin was on the other side. We get to our room and there are three bunk beds. We all run and grab our beds. Carl grabbed the bottom bed closest to the window. Joey pushed me out of the way so he could get the bottom bunk on the other side of the room. But I didn't care. I didn't mind being on the top bunk so I grabbed the one by the window so I could look out and think of her. We pull our things out of our bag. I flip through my poetry book, where I wrote my poems and copied poems of other poets I admired. I rip out a page, fold in and put it in my pocket.

Carl, Joey, Sticks and a couple girls from our school were the only people I knew at camp so I was excited to meet other people and learn about them. Ricky and Gordon were our cabinmates. They were more laidback than me. Ricky goes to Carver High School in Belmont. He plays soccer and is on the swim team. Gordon goes to Wesleyan Academy and is on the debate team. All he wanted to talk about was law school. I don't even know if Carl will graduate on time so any conversation about school was nipped in the bud immediately.

"So who's up for a friendly camp wager? I know I'm gonna win anyway but let's see who will be the first person to kiss a girl at camp." Carl said.

"I'm in!" Joey said.

Strutting in front of the other guys brushing his hair, Sticks chimes in. "So what do I win?"

Carl jumps off the bed and wrestles Sticks. He gets Sticks in a headlock and messes up his hair. He releases him and a smiling Sticks returns to brushing his hair.

Carl looks at me, Ricky and Gordon.

"Sure." Ricky said.

Carl looks at Gordon, then at me. Gordon looks at me and neither of us says anything.

"Everybody's in! So when we get to the all-camp meeting tonight, everbody can scope out their first victims and the game begins." Carl said.

Carl gets up and high-fives everybody, even though Gordon and I still hadn't agreed to participate. He knew that approaching girls was not my thing. Heck, I had a crush on Cindy Donnnely since the second grade and the most I had ever said to her was, "Yes," when she asked me if I could pass her homework up in Ms. Fenner's social studies class. But somehow I knew that I would connect to the girl that stepped off the bus. I don't know how but it was a feeling I had never felt before, not even the eight years of dreaming and fantasizing about Cindy Donneley.

That night at the barnfire, I spot her in the midst of about 200 campers. The counselors were giving us a rundown on activities and rules. Carl was pointing out girls to the rest of the guys. I couldn't hear anything they were saying. My eyes were fixed on her dark skin, her jet black hair, the best shape of any 14-15 year-old I had ever seen. It was something out of a movie. For the second time in a matter of hours, I experienced slow motion. And when she smiled... it was as if she was dancing on my heart, a whisper in my ear, telling me she loved me. I could feel myself smiling inside.

Carl nudges me. "You hear me? Did you see a ghost or

something?"

"An angel," I replied with a smile.

"Whatever!" Carl said. "Come on."

Everybody gets up and walks around, mingling.

Carl walks over to Gordon, who stands talking to three attractive girls.

"Gordon, you sly devil. I knew you were a playa!"

"Carl, this is Shelly, Nicole and Amber. They go to my school."

Carl extends his hand to Nicole. When she extends hers, he grabs her and pulls her close to him.

"I'm Carl. I'm really a hugger." He hugs Shelly and Amber as well. He turns to introduce the guys.

"This is Sticks. Joey... Where is Zack?" Carl said.

The men look around and they see me. They head in my direction. There I am conquering every fear I had ever had. I am standing in front of the most beautiful girl I had ever seen in my entire life. Her friend walks away, leaving me standing there with her as if we are alone on a beach under the stars with the ocean racing up to our toes and the sound of the waves providing a perfect bed of music for me.

I say to her, "Hello gorgeous, my name is Zachary Xavier Walton. From the moment I laid eyes on you, that marked the time that I started living. I felt a flutter in my heart that told me that you were the one I was born for. I knew that I had to come over and formally introduce myself to the girl I was destined to make happy for the rest of our lives. But before we get married, raise a family, and

live happily ever after, I, at least, should know your name."
She smiles and wraps her arms around me. I kiss her with
Carl, Joey, and Sticks looking on.

Ok, so maybe it didn't quite happen that way. But that's
how I envisioned it when I walked over to her in slow
motion. When I got there, I felt like I was in the second
grade. I reached into my pocket, took out the folded page I
ripped from the book, and handed it to her without saying a
word. Just like that. I walk away, never looking back,
hoping and praying I didn't stumble and fall and hoping I
didn't hear a chorus of laughter. I head straight past
everybody, directly to our cabin. I couldn't stand to see
what could happen.

The next day at breakfast, she came to our table and sat
beside me. She told me exactly what happened without
even telling me her name.

She said, "I watched you walk away, wondering if I was
being pranked or something. When I could no longer see
you, I sat by the fire and unfolded what I thought was a
note. I read, Annabel Lee by Edgar Allen Poe.

Annabel Lee
It was many and many a year ago
In a kingdom by the sea
That a maiden there lived whom you may know
By the name of ANNABEL LEE;
And this maiden she lived with no other thought
Than to love and be loved by me.

I was a child and she was a child

In this kingdom by the sea;
But we loved with a love that was more than love-
I and my Annabel Lee;
With a love that the winged seraphs of heaven
Coveted her and me.

And this was the reason that long ago
In this kingdom by the sea
A wind blew out of a cloud chilling
My beautiful Annabel Lee;
So that her highborn kinsman came
And bore her away from me
To shut her up in a sepulchre
In this kingdom by the sea.

The angels not half so happy in heaven
Went envying her and me-
Yes!- that was the reason (as all men know
In this kingdom by the sea)
That the wind came out of the cloud by night
Chilling and killing my Annabel Lee.

But our love it was stronger by far than the love
Of those who were older than we-
Of many far wiser than we-
And neither the angels in heaven above
Nor the demons down under the sea
Can ever dissever my soul from the soul
Of the beautiful Annabel Lee.

For the moon never beams without bringing me
dreams

Of the beautiful Annabel Lee;
And the stars never rise but I feel the bright eyes
Of the beautiful Annabel Lee;
And so all the night-tide I lie down by the side
Of my darling- my darling- my life and my bride
In the sepulchre there by the sea
In her tomb by the sounding sea.

For the moon never beams without bringing me
dreams
Of the beautiful Annabel Lee;
And the stars never rise but I feel the bright eyes
Of the beautiful Annabel Lee;
And so all the night-tide I lie down by the side
Of my darling- my darling- my life and my bride
In the sepulchre there by the sea
In her tomb by the sounding sea.

UNDER THE STARS

A deafening silence hovers over the therapist's office where Dr. Andrea Beckham waits for her client to gather herself and continue sharing. Valerie Stenson embraces the box of tissue like it's a baby, pulling one tissue at a time to wipe tears away and blow her nose. She enhales, slowly releases it and continues talking.

"I think my marriage is over," Valerie said. She struggles to continue. She tosses the used tissue in the trash can beside her, grabs several more from the box, and wipes away more tears. Andrea still doesn't say anything. "I don't know what to do. What am I supposed to do?"

Holding a blank notepad, Andrea leans forward in her chair. "Valerie, you've told me what happened with the rape. You've told me that you're afraid of losing your husband. You told me about the nightmares you have. But the one thing that you have yet to tell me is what you want?"

"That's the thing, Dr, Beckham. I don't know what I want. I thought I knew what I wanted." She pauses and blows her nose. "Yes, I do! I do know what I want. I want my marriage. I want my husband."

Valerie's husband, Miles, leaves the gym with his friends, Parker and Cortney. When they arrive at the parking lot, they talk while throwing their bags in the cars.

"Miles, I guess we'll catch you Monday," Parker said.

"What does that mean?" Miles responds. "It's Friday. You mean to tell me we're not doing anything this weekend?"

"*We* are," Cortney said with a chuckle. "Married men can't come out and play on the weekend without a permission slip."

"Whatever man!" Miles said. "What's the plan? I need to get out. The gym didn't quit do it for me, you know?"

Parker and Cortney look at each other in disbelief. "Well, we're hitting that new spot tonight," Parker said. "What's it called? 1202 or something like that?"

"1220! 1220 Peachtree!" Cortney said.

Miles gets excited. "Oh yeah! I heard about that spot. I heard the house band is awesome and the food is all that. I'm in."

"Cool, meet us there about 10," Cortney said.

"Bet!" Miles said.

The men get in their cars and pull off.

As he drives home in his convertible, Miles sings and dances to a Drake CD. He pulls up to a stop light and two women standing at the bus stop catch his attention. He smiles. Then waves. They return a smile. The car behind him blows the horn letting him know the light has changed. The women laugh and Miles waves again as he pulls off.

When he arrives home, he drops his bag just inside the door and kicks off his shoes. He hears Valerie in the kitchen. He sneaks up behind her and wraps his arms around her as she stirs a pot. She jumps.

"Something smells good!" he said as he nibbles on her ear.

She gathers herself and covers her nose. "It certainly is not you."

He turns her around and kisses her. He tries to grab the spoon behind her back and sneak a taste of her sauce. She catches him and takes the spoon.

"It's not ready yet."

"Are you? Cause I'm hungry, if you know what I mean."

She pulls away and turns back to stir the sauce. "Miles..."

He lets her go. As he turns to walk away, the smile fades and disappointment shows across his face. "I know. I know."

"Baby... I..."

Miles interrupts. "I'm going to take a shower." He turns back. "Oh, I'm going out with Cortney and Parker tonight."

When Miles leaves, she cries and slouches in a kitchen chair.

Upstairs, Miles stands at the closet in a towel, still damp from the shower. He matches shirts and pants trying to decide what to wear. Eventually he goes with the black and gray linen suit with a design on the shirt. He holds the shirt up to his chest in the mirror and nods in approval. As he splashes cologne on his face and neck, he notices Valerie standing at the door. He looks at her then returns to applying lotion. Valerie slowly walks over to him as he sits on the bed still wearing nothing but a towel. She stands in front of him and neither says anything. After a minute, Miles slides his hand up her shirt and feels her breasts. Valerie leans down and places her head on his head as he moves his hands around her waist. Her arms wrap around his neck and she holds his head.

When he tries to pull he pants down, she snatches back. In frustration, Miles shakes his head and grabs his deodorant and puts some on. Valerie takes the deodorant from him and puts it on the dresser. As she holds his thighs, she slides down on her knees in front of him, pulling the towel open. Miles strokes her head and slowly pulls her close to him.

Valerie has a flashback of being forced to perform oral

sex on her rapist just as she starts performing it on her husband. Miles falls back on the bed in frustration when Valerie stops. He jumps up, grabs his clothes and goes into the bathroom. He shuts the door behind him. Crying, Valerie runs out of the room. Miles opens the door when he hears her but she is gone. He goes back in.

Later that night, Miles drinks a glass of wine at the bar in 1220 while he waits for Cortney and Parker. At the other end of the bar, he sees two women looking in his direction. He quickly looks away and focuses on the sports on the television, never cracking a smile.

Cortney and Parker arrive and see him before he sees them. They walk up behind. Parker leans down behind Miles and whispers in a woman's voice, "Hey handsome, can I buy you a drink?"

Miles turns around and the men laugh.

"Did you tell Valerie you were taking the trash out and then peeled off?" Parker joked.

"Something like that," Mile said.

Cortney spots the two women who were checking out Miles. He waves and the women wave back. "It's going to be a fabulous night. I feel it," he said.

The men leave the bar and a hostess takes them to a booth. He hands the hostess the empty wine glass and asks for a shot of Ciroc for all three of them. Parker and Cortney look at each other then both look at Miles.

"Are we missing something?" Cortney asked.

"We're just gonna have a good time tonight," Miles said.

"Well that sounds like a good idea and an even better idea if you are paying," Parker added.

"On me tonight fellas." Miles said.

The server comes over with the shots. Each grabs one

and they hold them in the air.

"Here's to one helluva night." Miles said. The men down the drinks. "Another round!"

They get another round and down them as the band plays. Cortney gets up and tells Parker and Miles he'll be back. He walks over to the two women he saw when they first came in. Looking them up and down in their shirt, fitted dresses, he talks to them for a minute at the bar as Parker and Miles watch him.

Miles uses the opportunity to talk to Parker. "Can I ask you a question?"

"What if I say no?" Parker replied.

Miles, visibly tipsy at this point, shakes his head. "Let me rephrase that. I'm gonna ask you a question. And you are going to answer me." Miles laughs and Parker shakes his head. Then Miles gets serious again. "What am I doing wrong? What's wrong with me? I'm a good dude right?"

"Miles, what the hell are you talking about?"

"I   don't   know,   man."

"Dude, what's up?"

"It's Valerie. It's been eight months."

"Yeah, since the rape. I know you don't like talking about it. But you know I'm always here if you want or need to. I thought things were good, though."

"I ain't get none in eight months!"

Miles gestures to the server for more drinks. He tries to get something out of one of the empty glasses on the table. He gets a drop at best from one of the glasses.

"Man, I know that's gotta be tough bro," Parker said.

Miles looks around to make sure no one was listening. He leans closer to Parker. "I'm not gonna lie. It was tough for me at first to even kiss her or touch her. Every time I did, I thought about what that son-of-a-bitch did to her and I couldn't. But as time went on, I didn't see any of that. I just saw the woman I love and all I wanted to do was be there for her and make her happy and let her know that I'm there for her. I want to make love to my wife but she doesn't want any parts of that. Man, I am becoming a master masturbater!"

Parker chuckles and quickly stops. "You gotta remember the trauma she experienced. It's hard for her. She needs some time."

"I need some---"

Just then Cortney returns with the ladies from the bar. Parker tells Miles they'll talk later.

"This is Tessa and Imani. This is Parker and Miles."

Cortney directs them in the booth. They slide in next to Parker and Miles. Cortney sits on the end next to Tessa.

"Fellas, they are waiting on a friend so I told them they should come join us."

The server returns with the fresh drinks and Miles tells her to bring three more. He leans over to Parker and says, "I don't know if this is a good idea."

Back at their house, Valerie lay in bed watching television. She flips through the channels, apparently not interested in anything she pauses on. She stops of a re-run of Sanford and Son. She flips the channel to a movie, watches for a minute and changes the channel again. Judge Mathis catches her attention and she watches for a couple minutes. She glances up at the clock and it's 2:05 in the morning. She changes the channel and watches the Animal Channel. She looks at the clock again and it's 2:58. She falls asleep with the television watching her.

It's a little before 4 o'clock when Miles comes through

the door, quietly takes his shoes off, drops his keys on the table, and heads straight to the couch. He falls face first into the pillows. After adjusting himself, he drifts off to sleep.

The next morning as Valerie leaves for work, she bends down to kiss Miles and sees lipstick on his shirt. She stops halfway down and storms out of the door, slamming it behind her. The noise wakes Miles, who gathers himself and stumbles up the steps.

Valerie zones out as she sits in a conference room with about 10 other co-workers listening to a supervisor's presentation. Jennifer, her co-worker sitting next to her nudges her. She whispers to her. "Are you ok, Val?"

"Yeah I'm ok."

"Well, you should at least act like you are a little interested."

"Just got a lot on my mind. We'll talk during lunch."

"Ok."

Valerie and Jennifer walk across a street talking. They stop at a deli. They order soup, sandwiches and drinks and sit at a table in the corner of the room. They eat and talk.

"I knew you were going through a lot but I didn't realize things were that bad. I'm sorry." Jennifer said.

"I just don't know what to do," Valerie said, trying to fight back tears. "I think I might be driving him into the arms of other women."

"Don't assume that. A lot of times when we are stressed and things are in turmoil, we tend to think the worst. How long have you been married? Eight? Nine years? You've invested in each other. You love each other. You are just going through a rough patch. You can get through it."

Valerie wipes her eyes and blows her nose. "He had

lipstick on his shirt."

"And what did he say?"

"I didn't ask him."

"So don't read too much into it. You just need to talk to him. Let him know exactly what you are feeling and find out exactly what he is feeling. At least then you'll know what you are dealing with and you don't have to play the guessing game."

Valerie soaks in everything that Jennifer says. As she gathers herself, she takes a deep breath. "What am I paying Dr. Beckham for when I got you for free?"

"Oh, this isn't free. You will be paying for lunch for the next two weeks."

The women laugh. Valerie reaches across the table and hugs Jennifer. "Thank you."

Resting his head in his hands, Miles sits across the desk from Rev. Young in his office. The room is rather dark and gloomy. Rev. Young pours two glasses of water and hands one to Miles. "So what's going on son?"

"Pastor, I feel like everything is falling apart and I don't know how to stop it."

"Start from the immediate concern and go from there. What's troubling you the most?"

"My marriage."

"What about it?"

"Sometimes I blame myself for what happened to Valerie. I feel like maybe there was something else I could have done to prevent it. And other times I feel like there's nothing there. I mean I love her and I think she still loves me but I never imagined I could be married and be so lonely. Does that make sense? I know I'm not making any sense."

"Yes, Miles. I understand. I know it's not easy and Lord knows I don't have all the answers for you. But God does. The Bible says seek ye first the kingdom of God and his righteousness and and all the other things you want and need will be added unto you. Let him be your focus right now and be patient. He'll lead you. Trust him."

"I hear you, pastor. But we haven't been intimate since the rape. I'm not gonna lie, I've been tempted to do some things but I always remember what you said about not making decisions when you are emotional. I'm just weak right now. I'm confused and I just need some help. And to be honest, I don't know if I'll be able to keeping saying no."

"Let's pray, son."

Rev. Young stands, places his hand on Miles's head, and prays. When he is done, Miles stands and embraces him. He leaves the office.

In the car, Miles listens to Mary Mary's Go Get It. When he pulls up in front of his house, he shuts the car off and sits there for a minute with his eyes closed and his head back against the head rest. "I need you know Lord," he said.

Miles takes his time walking up the driveway and into the house. He gets inside, taking his shoes off at the door and walking into the kitchen. He pours himself a glass of water then makes his way upstairs where Valerie watches television in the bedroom. They barely look at each other. Miles takes off his watch and puts it on his dresser. He walks over and sits on the bed beside Valerie. He leans over and kisses her on the cheek.

"About last night..." he said.

"I don't even want to hear it."

"Nothing happened. I was drunk and... Val, nothing

69

happened. Come on."

Miles gets up and grabs her tennis shoes from the closet. He pulls her legs around and starts putting her shoes on her feet.

"What are you doing Miles?"

He gets one shoe on. "Just bare with me, ok?"

She helps him with the other one. He goes back to the dresser and puts his watch back on, grabs her by the hand and leads her down the steps. When they get to the door, he puts his shoes on and sends her out to the car. He jogs in the kitchen, grabs a bottle of wine from the refrigerator and two glasses. He puts them in a bag so she doesn't see them.

Valerie is already strapped in when he gets to the car. After getting in, starts it and pulls off. Mary Mary's Go Get It is on repeat in the car. About 10 minutes later, they arrive at a park.

"Why are we here?" Valerie said.

"Just come on."

They walk to a pavilion that has two picnic tables, a grill and a set of swings. Miles has the bag with the wine and a blanket. He lays the blanket on the ground and sits on it. Valerie sits as well.

"We need to talk and what better place for us to talk than the very place we met," Miles said. "First, let me get a sip of this wine." He pours a glass and hands it to Valerie, who appears angry and upset. He pours the second glass and downs the whole thing.

He continued. "Let me first say that I love you. I know that we've been through a lot lately but I hope that has never been in question. We've never really talked about what happened because it was difficult for both of us and I think since we didn't it made things worse. When you were violated, I was violated because that monster hurt the best part of me."

Miles tries to gather himself as tears fall. Valerie wipes the tears from her eyes as well.

"Val baby, I blamed myself for what happened and for a long time I didn't even know if I deserved you anymore. But I realized that we could make it through anything and I was ready to prove that. But when you continuously rejected me, I felt like you no longer wanted me." He takes a moment to gather himself, pouring another glass of wine and downing it. He exhales. "I don't know if God was testing my faith or punishing me. Yes, I've been tempting by other women and I've enjoyed the attention that I feel I was missing at home but you are the only woman I want. It's been that way since we met right here in this park and it's going to be that way for the rest of my life. I hope that's what you want, too. I understand if you need more time. I'm here and I'm willing to wait as long as it takes."

Valerie cries uncontrollably. She wipes her tears and blows her nose. Miles wipes his tears as well as he sips on another glass of wine. Valerie gathers herself, managing to say a few words at a time... "I do love you... I'm scared... I no longer feel pretty and I don't understand how God would let something like this happen... I dream of being intimate with you all the time but then the nightmare of what happened plays in my head. Then I wonder if you will even enjoy me that way anymore. What will happen if you don't?"

She stops and wipes her tears. Miles moves closer and puts his arm around her. Laying her head on his chest, she looks up at him. "Tell me you still think I'm beautiful."

"I tell you that all the time."

"I need to hear it now."

"You are the most beautiful woman I have ever seen in my life and I thank God that he blessed me with you." Miles holds her tighter, kissing her on the forehead. She kisses him on the lips, twice, the second time more passionately. Miles looks at her surprised then initiates the third passionate kiss. Valerie pushes Miles to the ground and climbs on top of him. They make love under the stars.

MAKING WINGS (SHORT STORY)

Janice consoles Stacey Farmington at the kitchen table. She goes to the refrigerator and pours a glass of water. When she closes the door, she notices a set of white wings on the refrigerator door, held by a magnet. She touches the wings and reads the writing stitched on one. It reads: "Mama's Angel, 5-9-13." She takes the angel off the door and brings it with her as she takes the water to Stacey, who is in pajamas for the third day in a row.

"Stacey, this is adorable. Did you make this?"

"No." said Stacey, taking a sip of water. But she doesn't immediately elaborate.

Stacey's baby was stillborn four days earlier. Even though she experienced complications throughout the pregnancy and doctors tried to prepare her for the worst, Stacey knew there is no preparation for the loss of a child. Stacey's grief is overwhelming. Because she was believing God for a miracle, she questioned him and became depression.

Janice, Stacey's best friend for 20 years, has been by her side throughout the pregnancy and the past four days. She was the one who helped Stacey name the baby, Angel Marie Farmington. So the angel wings were that much more significant to them both.

"Where did the wings come from?" Janice finally asks. "This is a sign from God that Angel is watching over you now. You have an angel in heaven."

Janice hands the angel wings to Stacey and strokes her back while Stacey stares at them. She rubs her finger across each side and slowly traces the lettering on the wings. She gets up and places the wings back on the refrigerator. They seemed to have calmed her a bit.

"When I got it in the mail, I did feel like God was watching over me," said Stacey, walking around the kitchen looking for something. "But sometimes the pain and the anger make me forget that he is there and that he does love me. I still can't understand why God would take my baby."

Janice leads Stacey back to the table and helps her sit down. "God is too big for us to understand him completely. But you know that he loves you and he obviously loves Angel enough to want her with him. Remember, she's with God and you'll always be her mother."

"All I know is every time I look up at those wings, I feel like Angel is here." Stacey said. "If that was the person's intent when they sent them then it worked. I would love to say thank you to them but there was no name or return address when it came."

"That's interesting," Janice said. "I thought you made it or someone we knew gave it to you. It has to be someone close to us. We should try to find out who it was and thank them."

"But they obviously wanted to remain anonymous."

"You do want to thank them right?"

"Yeah, I do."

"Come on."

Janice takes a picture of the wings with a small camera. She leads Stacey by the hand to the computer in the den, which is filled with balloons and cards, and connects the camera to the computer. They wait as it uploads. Janice signs into Facebook and puts the picture on her page.

"I'm going to tag you in it and see what happens,"

Janice said as she types, 'Someone sent these angel wings to Stacey. We would love to know who you are so we can thank you for your gesture of love. Get in touch with us or let us know how we can get in touch with you.' "We'll see what happens."

Later that day, Janice and a co-worker eat lunch at a local restaurant when she gets a phone call. She answers it and tells the person on the other end to hold on, and excuses herself from the table. She steps outside to take the call. The picture has gone viral, a friend tells her, and several other people in the city have received similar wings with the date that their loved ones passed. They, too, were trying to find the sender to thank them. Janice's face lights up as she gets off the call.

She sits on a bench and logs into Facebook on her phone. She scrolls through the comments and sees that the photo has hundreds of likes and dozens of shares. She immediately calls Stacey, who is sitting at the computer on Facebook when she answers the phone.

"Have you seen Facebook?" Janice asked.

"Yes, I'm looking at it right now," Stacey replied. "Janice, this is amazing! Whoever this person is is an angel herself."

"I'm going to come by later and we'll come up with a gameplan."

"Ok."

Stacey reads through the encouraging comments offering their condolences and prayers to her and others who have lost loved ones. She types… "If the person who sent the wings is reading this, thank you for what you've done. You've been a tremendous blessing to me and my family and to so many others." She pauses before sending the message but finally hits return and the message posts among the others.

Janice sits at her desk at work reading the stories about how people received wings and what they have meant to the families at some of the most difficult times they have ever experienced. Janice notices a familiar name, Sandy Alazar, a local television reporter whose son was killed in a horrific bus accident. She writes down Sandy's name and the television station on a piece of paper. She performs a Google search, finds a telephone number, and writes it on the paper as well.

Janice and Stacey drive to a local Internet café in the center of town where they meet a group of the family members who received wings. Six of them sit around the table, each with their wings. They pass them around so everybody can see the unique details to make them personalized, such as nicknames, stickers of the child's favorite sports balls, and dates. They talk about their experiences, including one woman who said receiving the wings kept her from committing suicide after the death of her daughter. Janice asks them if they would be willing to share their story with the media in an attempt to find this person and thank them. They agree.

She calls Sandy Alazar while they are there. After being placed on hold for a couple minutes and transferred, she finally gets Sandy.

"Hi Ms. Alazar. This is Janice Stansberry and I am here at Rosa's Café with six people who have received angel wings after the death of a loved one. I saw that you did as well after the death of your son. We were wondering if you would be interested in doing a story about the wings so that we can try to find the person who sent them."

"I think that's a great idea, but I know I wouldn't be able to do it," Sandy said. "I would be an emotional wreck. But let me talk to my assignment editor and see what we can do. What's your number? I'll get back to you after talking to him. But yeah, I think that'll be great."

Sandy discusses the idea with the news director, who doesn't see the news angle. But Sandy shared her son's story and how the wings had such an impact on her and so many others, the news director agrees and assigns the story to one of the other reporters for a weekend feature.

That weekend, the touching story airs with Stacey and two others being interviewed by the reporter. Each has their wings, showing where they keep them as reminders of their loved ones. One woman keeps it on her mirror so that every time she sees herself, she thinks about her angel. Stacey jokes that food is her comfort during her grieving period so that's why she keeps the wings on the refrigerator because she knows she will see them often.

The news is on in a hair salon and the story catches the attention of one of the stylists. She increases the volume and gets the attention of another stylist, who has angel wings pinned to her apron. She walks closer to the television and watches the story.

A man watching television at home writes down the website that scrolls across the bottom of the screen. A set of wings rests in the corner of a picture frame of a little girl about five years old.

A woman in her 30s watching the news is captivated by the story as she sits up in her bed. She smiles at Stacey's story. We see on her nightstand dozens of wings, glue, different color paints, and other supplies she uses to make the angel wings.

The reporter reminds the viewers of the website scrolling across the bottom that was set up to share stories about the wings and to help them find 'The Wing Maker' so they can show their appreciation.

The next day, the woman shops for supplies at the local craft store. When she reaches the checkout line, the cashier asked her if she watched the news over the weekend. The woman said no. The cashier smiled and said, "I finally know what you've been using all of these items for." The woman smiles back and puts her finger to her lips to tell the cashier to keep quiet.

The woman returns home and sits on the bed making more angel wings. She writes out a card that says, "God loves you and your baby." She places that with a set of finished wings and goes to the next one. There's a set of seven finished wings and cards on the bed and the woman continues to work on others.

The woman's husband enters the room with a laptop and sits on the bed with his wife. He pulls up the website and they read some of the posts and watch a few videos that people posted about the wings. They both cry and he comforts her.

"Honey, I think you should finally share your story," he said.

"Share our story?"

"Yes, our story."

She agrees to write a letter and send it to Sandy Alazar to share with the group.

> *Dear Loves,*
> *For 10 years I had been tormented by nightmares about my baby that died during birth. I blamed myself, wondering if it was because of something*

that I did during pregnancy, such as smoking and drinking, or if I was just being punished by God. Even though the doctors told me it wasn't my fault and that I was lucky to be alive, I still felt like I was responsible and that it should have been me instead of the baby who died. After receiving initial support from my immediate family, I felt like no one was there to support me in my difficult times. After two unsuccessful suicide attempts, I had the recurring, tormenting nightmare but this time it was interrupted by a good dream. In this dream, an angel came to me and told me that Baby Kiley is an angel now. She told me not to blame myself for what happened, that God had an assignment for her in heaven that only she could accomplish. She said that the reason I was still alive and couldn't kill myself is that I am still on assignment and my job is not complete. The angel left me a pair of wings and the message, "Angels are all around you."

I woke from the dream revived, refreshed, but trying to make sense of it. I went on a quest to figure out what my assignment was. I spoke with my husband and a couple of friends and no one could help me get clarity or understanding. But as I searched Craigslist, I stumbled across a woman who was seeking a support group for parents mourning the loss of a child. I used the woman's email address to find out who she was and where she lived. I went to the store, got the materials and made the first wings. I sent it to the woman. I then sought others and did the same. It made me feel good about myself and I never had the nightmares again. I knew

that my assignment was to help others. So I
continue to make angels for all of us. And I continue
to pray strength to each and every one of you. Love
you all,

     The Wing Maker

FATHER FORGIVE ME

Octavia crouches on the sofa frantically digging in her purse. She punches in a number and holds the phone between her face and her shoulder as she puts on a sheer, pink blouse to cover the sexy black bra she has on. Standing in a room spotlighted by the flicker of a near spent candle, she fastens her black jeans that snug perfectly to her voluptuous figure.

"Hey Kim, can I stop by? I really need to talk to you."

Kim cuddles in bed with a man as the phone wakes her. She looks at the clock to see it reads 12:17. "Hey O. Everything ok?"

"Yeah, I'm real good right now."

"Ok. I'll see you when you get here."

Octavia gathers her purse and keys from the coffee table. She tip-toes to the bedroom door and looks inside where a naked man sleeps on top of the covers. She shakes her head, bites her lip, and leaves.

A late model, red BMW coupe pulls up to a house in a suburban cul de sac. Octavia exits the car and makes her way to the door. Almost instantly after knocking on the door, Kim opens it and waves her in. Kim is wearing a white bathrobe and fluffy white slippers.

They sit on the couch in the living room, where Kim

hands Octavia a mug of coffee.

"I made a fresh batch. Sounded like you could use some," Kim said as she takes a sip of her own. "So what's going on that you had to see me so urgently at 1 o'clock in the morning. You're not running from the law are you?"

"The devil!" she replied digging in her purse and pulling out her phone. She scrolls through pictures.

"What?"

Octavia hands Kim the phone and she looks at the picture of a greased up, shirtless, dark-skinned man with a muscular build.

"Who is this?" Kim said, never taking her eyes off the phone.

"His name is Satan!"

Just then, Kim's husband Monty walks into the room. He closes his robe when he sees Octavia.

"Hey Octavia. I thought I heard another familiar voice down here. You ladies all right?"

Kim hands Octavia the phone back.

"Yeah we're good, honey. Octavia just needed to talk so I told her to come on over."

"Hi Pastor. Sorry to wake you."

"No, you're fine. I'm just going to grab some juice and I'll give you ladies some privacy. I just wanted to make sure everything was good."

"Thanks." Octavia said with a fake grin on her face. "See you Sunday."

"I'll be up soon, honey." Kim said as she and Octavia

watch Monty leave the room for the kitchen then upstairs. They wait an extra long time to make sure he was gone.

"Ok, so..." Kim said.

Octavia gets up and walks over to the doorway. She looks toward the steps to make sure Monty was gone. She pulls the picture back up on the phone. She hands it back to Kim who takes another look.

"That's Sheldon. He works in the office building next to the Starbucks. You know I have to get my latte every morning before I go to work. Well, I don't know if it's coincidence or not but I ran into him at least three times a week for the past two months. And one day he finally asked me out. It's been a long time since I've been on a date so I said, 'Why not?' So we go to the museum and to that Mexican restaurant down on 25th Street. Anyway, we had a great time so he asked me out again. So again I said, 'Why not?' He was a complete gentleman, we had natural chemistry, we had a lot in common and he was very pleasing on the eyes as you can see. Well, that second date was today."

Kim jumped in. "Did it not go well?"

"That's the problem. It went better than well. It was the most amazing night I had in a long time."

"And what's wrong with that. I don't hear a reason to call him Satan."

"When I say it was an amazing night, I mean it was an *amazing* night."

"Oh..." Kim gets up and walks to the kitchen. She

returns with the coffee pot. She pours some into their mugs. "I think we need to freshen these up."

They both sip some.

"I've been doing so well since coming back to the church," said Kim, with a look of disappointment on her face. "I really thought I would make it this time. I really thought I would remain celibate until married. Two years of faithfulness gone just like that."

"Octavia, let me talk to you for a minute as a minister and not as your friend. You know what the Bible says about fornication so I'm not going to preach to you. And the fact that you feel bad right now, you know that you shouldn't have done it. But God says that if you confess your sins, he will forgive you. The big part of repentance is the turning away."

Kim moves closer to Octavia and wraps her arms around her. Tears fall down Octavia's face. She tries to gather herself.

"Kim, I have known you for how long, about 15 years? You know me so I know I can be honest with you. I know right from wrong. But have you done something that was wrong but it felt so right? Everything about it felt right."

"But does it feel right right now?" Kim said.

"No," Octavia replied as she wept more under Kim's embrace.

Octavia, dressed in a casual business suit walks toward Starbucks. She spots Sheldon walking in her direction and slips into the flower shop next door before he sees her. She waits for him to leave before exiting the flower shot and going to Starbucks. She orders her latte and heads to work. Sitting in her cubicle, Octavia talks on the phone and takes notes. "Yes sir. We would love to develop a marketing campaign for your company. I'm sure we can put together a shell of a plan to give you an idea of what we can do for you. Yes sir. Thank you. I look forward to it."

Just as she hangs up the office phone, her cell phone buzzes and she glances at it. It's Sheldon. She hits ignore, sending it to voicemail. She waits, staring at the phone... until... the voicemail message indicator pops up. She punches in a number and listens to the message: "Good morning, Octavia. This is Sheldon. I was hoping I would run into you at Starbucks. Too bad for me I missed you. Anyway, I just wanted to say I had an amazing time last night and I was hoping I could see you again. Maybe Friday. Dinner. A movie. Maybe a walk in the park? Anyway, give me a call and let me know or hopefully I'll see you tomorrow morning for a Starbucks date."

Octavia smiles and leans back in her chair. She daydreams about making love to Sheldon the night before. Her fingernails dig into his back as he thrusts down on her. He grabs her hair and passionately kisses her neck and ear. They both moan. The phone rings, snapping her out of the daydream.

"Octavia Robinson. How may I help you?" she said as she fans herself.

Octavia, wearing jeans and a t-shirt, sits alone near the

back of the church during mid-week Bible study. About 75 people scattered about attend the service. Two young children run up the aisle and are snatched by a woman sitting about four rows from the altar. Kim, sitting in the front pew, spots Octavia and waves. Kim returns the wave and a smile as Monty teaches from the pulpit.

"Tonight we're going to be studying a familiar passage of scripture. If you have your Bibles, and I pray that we all come to church with the word because that's our primary weapon, turn with me to James Chapter 4 Verse 7. When you have it, say, 'Amen!'"

Pages turn and the congregation says, "Amen."

"I'll be reading from the New King James Version. 'Therefore submit to God. Resist the devil and he will flee from you.'"

Kim looks back at Octavia, who shakes her head and looks in another direction.

Monty walks down from the pulpit and stands at the altar in front of the congregation clutching his Bible. "What does it mean to submit to God? What does it mean to resist the devil? What does it mean when the Bible says the devil will flee from you? These are the questions we're going to answer tonight to help us with our Christian walk."

Octavia takes notes as Monty teaches. He phone vibrates in her purse. She digs for it, looks at it and sees that it's Sheldon calling. She hits the ignore button and places the phone back in her purse. She returns to note taking.

After the service, Octavia and Kim talk by the back

door.

"Kim, you didn't tell Monty about---"

Kim interrupts her. "Of course not! Have I ever violated our friendship? You know that your secrets are always safe with me. But God does have a way of speaking directly to our situations. We all needed to hear that word."

"I know I sure did," Octavia said. "It helped a lot. He actually called me in the middle of service too."

"Who God?" Kim said with a laugh.

"No, Sheldon."

"Maybe that was the sign you needed so you can resist the devil."

"I guess you're right."

"Well, I'm glad you made it tonight. Call me tomorrow."

"I will. Tell Monty I said bye."

The next day as Octavia stands in line waiting on her latte, Sheldon, decked out in an expensive suit, walks up behind her, wraps his arms around her waist and whispers in her ear. "Is this what a man has to do to get your attention? Stalk you in Starbucks."

Octavia smiles buts gently pulls away. "No, no at all. But having a latte as a conversation starter is not a bad idea."

"Have you gotten my messages? I've been calling you all week. Did I do something wrong?"

Octavia gets her latte and walks away from the counter with Sheldon in pursuit. "No you didn't," Octavia said. "I've just been busy and dealing with a few things I need to take care of."

"Can you slow down for a minute so we can talk?"

"I'm sorry, Sheldon. I have to run."

Sheldon grabs her by the arm. "Hold up. I have something that I've been carrying around with me until I saw you." He reaches in his jacket pocket and pulls out a miniature sombrero. "You forget this last weekend. I figured if you keep it around, you'll think about me from time to time."

Octavia takes the sombrero and turns and walks away. When she gets a few steps from him, she smiles but doesn't let Sheldon see her. He calls her. "Octavia!" and she turns without smile. "That date request for Friday still stands." She turns back and keeps walking.

Back in her cubicle, Octavia places the sombrero on the shelf, right at eye level. She smiles.

It's Friday night and Octavia, standing in the hallway of Sheldon's apartment, wears black jeans, a red blouse, and sexy red boots. Sheldon yells from the bathroom. "Sorry I'm running a little late. Got off work later than I expected. But I won't be long, I promise." Octavia doesn't say anything. "Make yourself at home, fix a drink, turn on the television, whatever. Mi casa es su casa!"

Octavia mumbles to herself... "Resist the devil and he will flee..." She walks to the door, turns the knob and opens it. She looks out. Then closes it. Sheldon hears the doors close. "Octavia! Is that you?"

"Yeah, it's me. I'm still here."

"I thought you were trying to run away from me."

Mumbling to herself again, "Yeah... I was."

Sheldon emerges from the bathroom with nothing but a towel around his waist, water dripping from his body. Octavia takes a deep breath and slowly exhales. She knows that she should go. Her body quivers. She turns and looks into his eyes. Then at his lips. And his wet chest. He remains silent as he looks her up and down. She quickly looks away and heads to the door. With her right hand she grabs the doorknob... Twists twice. Her left hand slowly slides up the door feeling for the deadbolt. She locks it, mumbles, 'Father, forgive me,' and heads back in his direction.

SWAG

The first day Juan came to Kim's office it was above 90 degrees and the air conditioning was out. Crews had been there all day working on it but nothing seemed to work. It looked more like a sweat shop than an upscale marketing and promotions company. Fans were going everywhere, including people holding small personal fans and desktops fans.

In walks Juan, as if the mood was set just for him and his tank top showcasing his chiseled physique. His walk was almost as rhythmic as the dance moves he's known for. All the ladies in the office watched him as a receptionist directed him to Kim's office. It was something out of a bad porno, the way he slowly walked toward her and all eyes followed him. He wiped sweat from his face as he talked to his assistant along the way.

When he finally reaches her, Kim is struck by his attractiveness. She fans herself faster, blaming it on the heat. He's about 10 years her junior and maybe that was a little bit of the attraction, too. He was charismatic and charming and had what the young people call swag. They shake hands and he tells her: "I'll have to come back later 'cause it's hotter than a whorehouse in Texas." Kim's forehead wrinkled not knowing what to make of his analogy.

"And just how do you know that?" she asked, focusing in on his lips waiting for a response.

He turns to his assistant and chuckles. "Maybe I heard." They all laugh and exchange business cards. Kim tells him she'll call to set an appointment once the AC is fixed.

91

"Don't keep me waiting too long," he said. He winks at her and turns and walks away.

The office is abuzz as the women continue fanning themselves. They gather in small cliques pointing as Juan and his assistant walk to the elevator.

"I see you got a new boyfriend," said Paula, Kim's best friend and co-worker. "Your husband is going to kill the both of you."

"Girl please," Kim said. "My man has nothing to worry about."

"Have you seen his dance moves?" Paula asked. "That's swag. That's enough to make me worry. That body... umpf!"

Kim fans herself again. "Girl, you need to stop it."

"Oh, you're hot now, huh?"

The women laugh as Paula leaves Kim's office.

Just then, the air conditioner kicks on and everybody on the floor claps.

Kim calls Juan to let him know that the air conditioning was fixed and he can stop back up later he if he has an opportunity. But he tells her that he has to prepare for a class and that they can schedule it for another time or she could swing by the studio. She chose the studio.

Kim finds Paula and tells her that she's going to meet Juan at his studio to discuss his marketing campaign needs.

When Kim arrives at the studio, she looks at the competition awards and trophies in a display case. She walks through the hallway and looks at every picture on the wall, most with Juan and his students at dance competitions, video sets and award shows. Juan spots her and watches her from the end of the hall without her seeing him. When she finally notices him, she blushes.

"I see you found it. Let me give you a quick tour," said Juan, leading Kim through the various classrooms.

"You're Canadian, right," Kim asks.

"Yes, I am." he said.

"I didn't realize Canadians had accents."

"It depends on what part of the country you're from. Same as in the U.S., where you have your New England accent and your Southern drawl. If you are from Vancouver, you sound different than if you're from Toronto and they sound different from other parts."

"You learn something new every day," she said.

"That's just the beginning of what I'm going to teach you."

"Is that right?"

"That is absolutely right."

He walks away and into a room. She fans herself just like she did in the office except the studio is nice and cool. Unbeknowst to her, he watched her on the monitors in the room. He turns on some music and heads back to the main dance studio with Kim.

"I'm working on choreography for a group. I'm gonna show you a couple moves," he said as he pulls her from the chair she tried unsuccessfully to cling to.

"Ah, I don't think that's a good idea." she said, still trying to make her way to the chair.

"Why is that?"

"I haven't danced in years and you don't want me to tell anybody I am one of your students. You might lose business."

"I'll take my chances."

"So you're a gambling man?"

"If the stakes are high enough."

He scoops her up and carries her to the middle of the dance floor. Her resistance settles and becomes more of a blush. He puts her down and stands behind her, grabbing her waist and twisting her hips to the bass-driven beat.

"First thing you gotta do is feel it," he said.

She closes her eyes and takes over the motion Juan started.

"That's it. That's it!" he said.

He lets her go and she continues. He walks in front of her.

"Now watch this then jump in. 1, 2, 1, 2, 3, 4..."

He goes hard, moving side to side, jirating, pumping his fists in the air, kicking... Kim busts into laughter and sits on the floor. They laugh.

"I'm just playing. Com'on," he said.

He helps her to her feet and starts a simple two-step to get the rhythm then walks her through a few simple moves. She messes up a few times and he holds her waist to demonstrate the movement and grabs her arms to show her how to pump her fists in the air. They laugh. The playfully push each other and finally, a small embrace. After a brief, awkward moment, Juan leaves to turn off the music. When he returns, Kim is gathering her things.

"So you have a better idea of the dance studio what I do and what I need, right?" he asks.

"Yeah, I think I do," she said as she blots the beads of sweat from her forehead with a paper towel.

"Well, if you feel like you need anything else, I'm always here. I practically live here. Or if you need another dance lesson or two, you know where to find me."

Kim fans herself with the unfolded paper towel.

"I see you are a glutton for pain. That sad attempt at

dancing didn't traumatize you?"

"Not even!"

"Ok. I hear you Mr. Kelly."

As Kim drives back to work, a smile is glued to her face. She thinks of was Juan's hands around her waist and that awkward embrace as she stumbled into him. It was the best day of "work" she had in a very long time.

Later that evening at home, Kim and her husband, Jay, sit at the kitchen table eating dinner. Jay spots files and two CDs on her laptop. He recognizes one of them.

"When did you become a Lil Skee fan?" he said sarcastically.

"How do you know Lil Skee?" she replied.

"Sometimes I feel like I have to be a hip hop expert to reach my students. Compare something to a rapper or a rap song and they will pick it up in a heartbeat. Tell them to just read something and get the meaning… it's a lost cause. So they keep me well informed about Lil Skee, Shorty Do-Do, Stinky Stank Stank and 'nem."

They chuckle as Jay's attempt at rap impersonation and improvised rap names fall short.

"I have a new client I'm developing a marketing campaign for who is actually doing choreography for Lil Skee and a few other rappers and their dancers," Kim said. "So I'm trying to learn a few things."

"Maybe he can get one of the rappers to stop by the school sometime to speak with the kids. I'm sure I'll get some cool points for that."

"I'll run it past him. Can't hurt to ask, right?"

"Right!" Jay said while chewing.

Juan enters Kim's building. The receptionist sends him to Kim's office and she closes the door behind him. They talk and she is all smiles. He stays for just a few minutes and leaves. She watches him leave, as do the other women in the office.

At Jay's school, Lil Skee talks to a group of students in a classroom. Jay sits in the back of the class watching as the students give their full attention to the rapper, who hands each of them a CD. When he gets done, they all clap and Jay takes pictures of each student with Lil Skee.

Later that night, Jay and Kim sit on the couch watching television. Jay tells her that he is now the coolest teacher in the building. He thanks her for helping him get Lil Skee to speak to the students.

Several days later, Juan and Kim meet at a restaurant for lunch. She hands him a folder. As he grabs the folder, he holds onto her hand. They look into each other's eyes briefly and Juan releases her hand. She looks around to see if anyone caught that moment.

As Kim talks on the phone in her office, Paula walks in.

"Is that Juan?" Paula said.

Kim shakes her head yes and Paula shakes her head no and leaves.

At Jay and Kim's house, Jay is asleep with his head on Kim's lap. The television is on but Kim is engulfed in her phone. She smiles as she sends text message after text message. She glances down from time to time at Jay to make sure she isn't waking him. She doesn't notice him peeking up at her from time to time either. After a while texting, she sets the phone on the nightstand. Minutes later she picks it up and looks at it with a blank stare. A few more minutes pass and she does it again. And yet again. She looks a little confused, obviously awaiting a response.

Kim falls asleep without getting the text she was waiting

on.

Several hours later she's awakened by a car pulling into the driveway. The clock reads 2:12 a.m. Kim slides Jay off her without waking him and looks out the window. She's shocked as she sees Juan's car. As she rushes down to try to get him away from the house, Jay wakes up. Juan stumbles out of the car and yells Kim's name. Kim gets outside and tries to keep Juan quiet. She looks up at the bedroom window to see if Juan woke Jay up.

"Juan! What are you doing here!?!" she said as she pushed him back to the car. "You need to get out of here right now before Jay wakes up."

"But I need you Kim. You hear me? I need you!" he replied.

He tries to hug her as she tries to get him back in the car.

"Go home, Juan! Now!"

"Kim...? Kim....?"

"What!?!"

"I love you!"

Kim doesn't reply. She pushes him all the way in the car and closes the door.

"Kim... I said I love you."

"Go!"

Juan swerves off. Jay comes outside, fully dressed with a gun in his hand. He approaches Kim.

"What the hell!?!" he said.

"That was one of my clients. There was an emergency. Everything is ok. Let's just go back to bed."

"Back to bed my ass!"

He pulls her phone from his pocket and shoves it to her stomach.

"I should..." He stops mid-sentence and puts the gun in

97

his waistband. He pulls keys from his pocket and briskly walks towards his car.

"Baby, wait! Where are you going?" she said as she tries to prevent him from getting in the car.

He turns to Kim and with a calm, quiet voice he says: "If you are smart, you will take your hands off me and take your ass in the house."

Kim lets go and backs up.

"Jay… Jay…"

He ignores her. He gets in the car and peels off.

Kim runs back in the house. She sits on the bed and looks at her phone. She reads the most recent messages:

Juan - 1:47 a.m. – "I'm omw ova there!"

Juan – 1:43 a.m. – "I need to talk to you."

Juan – 1:35 a.m. – "Where are you. say something"

Juan – 1:34 a.m. – "Did you get my last message?"

Juan – 1:22 a.m. – "You miss me and I luv you"

Kim – 1:05 a.m. – "I miss you. Can't wait to see what you are going to teach me next?"

Juan – 1:03 a.m. – "Me too"

Kim – 1:02 a.m. – "I love the way you make me feel.

Juan – 1:00 a.m. – "Is that all? lol"

Kim – 12:57 a.m. – "Your body's aight too lol"

Kim – 12:56 a.m. – "I like your confidence, your swag as you say"

Kim – 12:55 a.m. – "I like the way your lips curl when you smile. I like the way you laugh when you think you are funny."

Kim – 12:53 a.m. – "I like the way you dance. I like your accent lol"

Juan – 12:51 a.m. – "What do you like about me?"

Kim sets the phone down beside her.

"Damn!"

She falls back on the bed then springs up in a panic. She grabs the phone and punches in a number. "Paula, sorry to wake you up. I messed up. I messed up big time."

"You all right? What's going on?"

"Jay just left the house with his gun and I think he might be going after Juan."

"What? On my God! What happened?"

"Long story short... Juan came by the house a little while ago drunk talking about he loves me and I think Jay read text messages me and Juan sent each other."

"Oh my God! Oh my God! Did you try to call him?"

"Who Juan?"

"No! Jay... to try to calm him down?"

Kim looks over sees Jay's phone on the dresser.

"I was going to but he left his phone here. I'm scared Paula. I don't know what he's going to do?"

"What would you do in that situation? Exactly! You need to call Tony and see if Tony can catch up with Jay and talk to him before he finds Juan."

"Ok. Let me call Tony now. I'll keep you posted."

"Ok. Call me back."

"I will."

Tony tries a few places he thinks Jay might be but has no luck. He tells Kim if he hears anything he'll let her know.

In the meantime, Kim goes through Jay's phone hoping she'd find communication between Jay and another woman to make her feel better about what she's been doing with Juan. But she found nothing other than a few harmless comments of pictures where women said he was attractive. It made Kim feel worse. But she also wondered if he

99

cleared his phone or if all the things she had thought about him possibly doing was only fuel to justify what she wanted to do.

Jay pulls into a school parking lot. The gun sits in his lap. He lays his head on the steering wheel then gets out of the car, placing the gun back in his waistband. He walks down the street, still visibly upset.

Somehow he ends up at the local diner, talking to Tasha, his ex-girlfriend. He vents everything to her in a drunken confession. Tasha calls Kim to let her know he's there and that he's all right.

As Kim drives to the diner, she fears what could happen. When she arrives, she spots Tasha and Jay sitting in a booth. His head is on the table. Tasha walks over to Kim and they sit in another booth. Tasha has a cup of coffee and Kim orders something to drink.

"Thanks for calling me," Kim said. "I know this is awkward given your past with him and knowing how I feel about you."

"I'm not the enemy, Kim. Never has been. I'm just looking out for the both of you. He got here and called me. And as drunk as he was, I knew you needed to know where he was."

"I appreciate that. But this doesn't mean we're girls or nothing like that. I still don't care for you."

"What Jay and I had was long before the two of you were involved. And to be honest, I messed that up," Tasha said, appearing sad. "Jay was only concerned about making me a better woman. That was all he ever asked of me... was for me to be better for myself. He was the first gentleman I ever met."

"I've always heard things about you and wondered how

I would feel when I finally met you." Kim said.

"What did you think?"

"I thought I would want to kill you."

"Why?"

"Because I always felt like he settled for me and that you are the one that he really wanted to be with, kinda like the one who got away," Kim said, taking a sip of her water to gather her emotions. "Whenever I wanted to really be angry with him, I'd think about him making love to you and him wishing he was with you instead of me. I can't believe I'm actually telling you this."

"Wow! Jay is a great friend. I owe him everything but I know if I had the world to offer him, he wouldn't accept it. He'd find a way to give it back to me and show me how to enjoy it in a way that I never knew before, like I never had it before. Like I said that was long before you were involved."

Kim appears in deep thought, occasionally glancing over at Jay. "So your son is not Jay's?"

"Kim, Jay loves you. He loves you more than anything," Tasha said.

Kim hangs her head in shame as she thinks about what's been going on with Juan. "Thank you."

Kim walks over to the booth where Jay is and wakes him.

"Tasha…" Jay said, struggling to adjust his eyes to the light.

"No, it's me, baby," Kim said.

"Kim, what are you doing here?"

"I came to get my husband. Come on. Let's go home."

Jay tries to stand and stumbles into the table. "Yeah, let's go home."

Kim helps Jay out of the diner and into the car. She drives him home, helps him out of the car and into the house. When they get in the door, Jay stares at Kim.

"What?" she asks.

"I got swag!" he said.

"Yes, you do baby!"

THOUGHTS OF A DEAD MAN

Nathan Nicholson buttons his white oxford shirt in the exam room at his doctor's office. He sits on the exam table and slides his lizard skin shoes on his feet. He stands and tucks his shirt in his pants then walks around the room looking at pamphlets and pictures on the wall. Back to the exam table he goes, looking around like he'll find something new. Hopping down from the table again, he walks over to the sink to wash his hands and returns to the table. He takes his phone out and scrolls through messages.

Dr. Jung, carrying a clipboard and a prescription pad, enters the room along with an assistant who closes the door and has a seat in a chair near the door.

Dr. Jung writes on the prescription pad, tears two off and hands them to Nathan. He places his hand on Nathan's shoulder and gives him some obvious bad news as Nathan's head hangs. Dr. Jung and his assistant leave Nathan in the room alone again. A tear falls from Nathan's eye. He lay back on the exam bed. After a serious of deep breaths, Nathan gets up, wipes his face and leaves the office.

Nathan enters Joey's, the neighborhood pub he frequents, and walks over to the bartender calling his name. With a huge grin on his face, he walks over and shakes hands with some of the people sitting around the bar. He reaches across the bar and hugs the bartender.

"Let me get a couple beers, Vince," Nathan said. "I'll be in the back. So if you see Ben come in, let him know for me."

"Will do," Vince said as he hands Nathan the beers.

"Hey, do you have a pen and some paper?" Nathan said.

"Sure do." Vince turns and grabs a note pad and a pen from a shelf. He hands them to Nathan.

"Thanks buddy." Nathan said.

Nathan sits in a booth writing. He sips on his beer, occasionally staring at the other patrons in the pub, sometimes just staring at the walls, obviously in deep thought. Ben plops down across from Nathan, knocking him out of his daze. He grabs Nathan's beer and takes a sip.

"I see you got started without me," said Ben, sliding the beer back to Nathan. "I ordered us a pitcher." On cue, a waitress brings a pitcher of beer and places it on the table in front of the men. Nathan uses the opportunity to hide the notepad on the seat beside him.

"You need a menu Ben? I already know what Nathan wants," the waitress said.

Ben mean-mugs Nathan. "And you ordered without me?" he said. "That's some bull!" The men laugh. "Let me get a cheeseburger and fries, no onions though."

"Coming right up," she replied.

Ben watches her walk away in her tight jeans. "This is exactly why I love this place. The scenery is incredible." He turns back to Nathan and pours himself a beer.

"So what's up Nate? How is the firm treating you these days?" Ben said.

"Good. You know... it's work. But I took the day off to

take care of some business. Had a few appointments. What about you?"

"I put my time in at the plantation and called it a day."

"You still have your vacation set for the second week in June right?"

"Sure do. I don't know what I'm gonna do except stay the hell away from that place."

Nathan reaches in his pocket and pulls out an envelope and puts it on the table in front of Ben.

Lifting the envelope up and inspecting it, Ben says, "What's this?" Nathan laughs.

With a grin, Nathan tells him to open it.

Just as Ben goes to open the envelope, the waitress brings their food. She slides the plates in front of the men. Ben stares at Nathan's plate, which is twice the size of his cheeseburger and fries.

"Hungry are we?" Ben chuckles. The waitress smiles. Without adding any condiments, Nathan picks up a massive burger that is too big for the bun. He bites into it and lettuce and tomatoes fall to his plate.

"Now that's what I'm talking about," Nathan says with a full mouth.

Ben puts the envelope on the seat beside him and takes a bite of his burger. It's far cleaner than Nathan with no spillage. "Why do I feel like I'm missing something," he said. He pours ketchup on the burger. He takes another bite. "That's better but I want mine to run down my face like yours."

They men laugh. Nathan hasn't said much since diving into his food. He washes it down with beer. He dramatically swallows and gathers himself. "Are you going to open it?" he said, pointing in the direction of the envelope.

Reaching for the envelope, Ben said, "Oh yeah, you distracted me with that Braunesaurus burger."

Nathan goes for more food, watching Ben open the envelope. Ben's eyes light up as he pulls out a plane ticket. "What!?! Honey Hawaii?" The most beautiful place in the world and the home of the most beautiful women in the world?"

Nathan puts down his burger and walks around the table and hugs Ben. "You always wanted to go, so we're going."

"Wow. I don't know what to say," Ben said. "Yes I do! We going to Hawaii! Whooooooooo!"

In Hawaii, Nathan and Ben lay out on beach with drinks in the hands. Beautiful women walk past and the men soak up the views with the blue ocean as a backdrop.

"You know me so well," Ben said as his head swivels to see which beautiful woman his eyes will follow down the beach. "This week has been the best gift I have ever received. If you were one of these women, I would kiss you."

"Ben, I need to tell you something."

"You got more surprises?"

"Well... sort of. I need your help."

"After this, anything! What's up?

"There really is no easy way to say this. I've tried to find the best words and practiced in my head but it hasn't helped."

"Nate, what's going on? You starting to kill my buzz."

"I'm sick. I don't have long."

"What!?! What are you saying bro?"

"The cancer is back. Doctors said I probably have eight months."

Nathan stands and starts walking down the beach. "Nah man! No!" He paces a few yards from Nathan who holds his head in his hands. Ben returns, wiping tears from his eyes.

"We can beat this, right?" Ben said, trying to gather his thoughts and choking up with every word. "We can get a second opinion, right? We got the best doctors in Atlanta. There gonna make sure you're ok, right? Man!"

Nathan stands and embraces Ben, who finally lets out his tears. Nathan doesn't. "Come on man. Sit down and have a drink. I really need to talk to you," Nathan said.

The men sit back down. Ben finishes off his drink with one gulp. Nathan hands him another drink.

"The reason I wanted to bring you here to Hawaii is because I knew it was always a dream of yours and as my best friend, I wanted you to be the first person to know," Nathan said in a calm monotone voice. "I don't want anybody else to know."

"But..."

Nathan, not allowing Ben to jump in, interrupts him.

"Just like this was a dream of yours, I want to fulfill dreams of the other four people who mean the world to me... my grandmother, my sister, my mentor and Erica. I want... I need your help on this. Can I count on you?"

Ben gathers himself. He takes another drink before responding. "Of course, you can count on me. We're not just friends; we're brothers." Ben pauses. "But Erica?" Nathan laughs and Ben manages a chuckle through the emotion.

Grandmother

A salesman hangs three fur coats on a rack... one white with grey and black streaks, one black, and one brown. They are different lengths and styles. Nathan looks them over and the salesman points out features on each of them. Nathan points for the salesman to remove the black one. He holds the other two up. He stares at them for a minute, finally deciding on the white one. Nathan follows the salesman to the register to pay for the coat. After paying and the salesman places the coat in a carry bag, Nathan leaves the store.

Nathan knocks on the door of his grandmother's house. The 76-year-old woman opens the door and gives him a huge smile, followed by a hug and a kiss on the check.

"Nathan, baby! It's so good to see you," she said as she held the door open for him to come in.

"You doing all right, grandma?"

"Grandma's doing just fine."

"You looking good."

"Well what else am I supposed to look like?"

"Just like that, grandma. Beautiful, just like that."

She motions for him to sit on the couch. He lays the coat across the back of another chair and sits on the couch.

"What in the world is that?" she said.

"Just a little something I got for you," said Nathan, popping back up to take the coat out of the carry bag. He holds it up so she can see it. "This is for you grandma. I know you always said one day a man would buy you a fur. So I'm that man."

"Oh my!" she said, as she rubbed her hand up and down the coat. "How in the world did you remember that? You were just a boy when I said that."

"I never forgot." Nathan helps his grandmother put the coat on. "I always wanted to be the one who got it for you. And look at you. You look like a movie star."

Nathan sits back on the couch and watches his grandmother pose in the mirror with her coach on. She turns to the left, then to the right. She turns her back to the mirror and looks over her shoulder. She smiles.

Mentor

Daniel Witaker enters his office at Van Buren, Witaker, and Fountaine Attorneys at Law. He drops his briefcase beside his desk, sits down and sorts mail. He tosses some to the side, puts a few in the shredder by his desk, and opens one. He reads it and puts it aside. When he looks up, he spots The Birth of Venus, the 1486 painting by Sandro Botticelli that depicts the goddess Venus emerging from the sea as an adult woman, arriving at the seashore.

"How did this get here?" he said to himself as he rushed over to the painting. He grabs a letter taped to the frame. He admires the painting before returning to his desk then sits down and reads the note.

"I could never thank you enough for all you've done for me, including giving me my first internship while I was in college and hiring me even before I passed the bar. You are the best mentor a man could ever have. I know the Birth of Venus is your favorite painting. So consider this my thanks for always being there for me. And no, I didn't steal it. Nathan."

Daniel smiles. He walks back to the painting.

Sister

Nathan and Jason, his brother in-law, purchase corn dogs from a street vendor. After paying and putting condiments on them, they walk through the park, talking.

"Jason, I need your help with something," Nathan said as the men approach a bench and have a seat.

"Sure, what do you need?" Jason said.

"You know how Cynt always wanted to go skydiving and laughed because I said I would never do it? Well, I want to surprise her and go skydiving with her."

"You want to go skydiving?" Jason laughs.

"No. I want to go skydiving with her," Nathan said. "We have a lot of memories from our childhood but since our parents died we went our separate ways. She married you and started a family and we just haven't had many moments and I want to do this."

"I think that's awesome," Jason said. "I think she'll love that. So what do you need me to do?"

"Set it up as if just the two of you are going and I will surprise her there," Nathan said. "You can't let her know."

"I can do that," Jason said.

"Thanks."

Jason and Cynthia enter the skydiving training session where a dozen other people sit around the simulation room waiting for the instructor. They have on all of their equipment, including their parachutes and goggles.

"Am I really about to do this?" she said smiling.

"You sure are," Jason replied.

Out of the corner of her eye, she spots someone walking towards them. He takes his goggles off and she recognizes Nathan.

"Oh my God! Nate, what are you doing here?" said Cynthia, jumping in Nathan's arms.

"Hey Pumpkin!" Nathan said. He kisses her on the cheek. He shakes Jason's hand and winks at him. "Jason."

"Are you diving? No way!" she said, answering herself before he could.

"It's me and you baby girl!" Nathan said.

Jason takes off his equipment and gives her a kiss. "Have fun, Sweetie. See you when you touch down."

"Oh my God!" she said, hugging Nathan again.

"Surprise!" Nathan said.

The plane's door opens. Nathan stands there with his

instructor behind him and Cynthia with her instructor behind her. They look at each other. "You ready?" Nathan asks.

"Are you?" she replied.

"Absolutely!"

"Here we go," Nathan's instructor said. "One, two, three..."

Nathan and Cynthia look at each other and give each other a thumbs up and off they go, screaming in excitement as they soar through the air.

Three months later, Nathan lost his battle with cancer. At his funeral, all of the people who meant something to him attended. Ben walked around the room handing out the letters that Nathan wrote to them. He gave one to his grandmother. Cynthia. Then Jason. Finally, Ben finds Erica, Nathan's ex-girlfriend who seemed to be taking the death hardest.

Erica

"Hi, Erica. You ok?" Ben asked.

"Yeah. I'll be ok Ben. Thanks," she said, wiping tears from her eyes.

Ben sits next to Erica. "I know you and I haven't always seen eye-to-eye," he said. "But we both loved Nate and he loved both of us. I made him a promise that I would make sure you got this."

Ben hands Erica a package. He looks over at Cynthia, Jason and Nathan's grandmother, who are all crying and consoling one another while reading Nathan's letters. Erica opens the package and finds a custom jewelry box that looks like a globe. Inside is a diamond, heart-shaped necklace. Ben helps her put the necklace around her neck. Tears fall from her eyes again. She opens the letter and reads it.

"Erica, I promised you the world and was never able to give you that. I'm sorry. My hope is that you experience everything you ever want in life. Don't take life for granted because you never know when your time is up. I took a lot for granted, including you. I hope you can find it in your heart to forgive me. And although I am gone, you have always had and always will have my heart. I love you, Nathan."

ABOUT THE AUTHOR

C. Nathaniel Brown is an award-winning writer, publisher, and writing coach. He is author of five successful books, including Xs, Os, and Ws: Inspirational Stories from Successful Basketball Coaches; Devil in the Mirror: Overcoming the Enemy's Attack; and The Business of My Book, a guide to help writers understand the business side of writing. As a writing coach, he assists writers develop concepts, overcome writers block and navigate through the publishing process. He resides in Atlanta, Ga.

OTHER TITLES

BY C. NATHANIEL BROWN

- ✓ I Always Put the Seat Down
- ✓ Devil in the Mirror: Overcoming the Enemy's Attack
- ✓ Xs, Os, and Ws: Inspirational Stories from Successful Basketball Coaches
- ✓ The Business of My Book: Making More Money and Reaching More People by Understanding the Business of Being a Writer
- ✓ The Hair Commandments: Shalls and Shall Nots of Wigs, Weaves, Bald, and Natural Hair (with LaToya Johnson-Rainey)
- ✓ No Timeouts (Coming Fall 2014)

For more information or to order these titles, visit www.EX3ent.com

www.ingramcontent.com/pod-product-compliance
Lightning Source LLC
Chambersburg PA
CBHW071405170626
46811CB00003B/1262